Mischievous Mosquitoes

Kelly Doudna

Consulting Editor, Diane Craig, M.A./Reading Specialist

visit us at www.abdopublishing.com

Published by ABDO Publishing Company, a division of ABDO, P.O. Box 398166, Minneapolis, Minnesota 55439. Copyright © 2012 by Abdo Consulting Group, Inc. International copyrights reserved in all countries. No part of this book may be reproduced in any form without written permission from the publisher. SandCastle™ is a trademark and logo of ABDO Publishing Company.

Printed in the United States of America, North Mankato, Minnesota
102011
012012

 PRINTED ON RECYCLED PAPER

Editor: Katherine Hengel
Content Developer: Nancy Tuminelly
Cover and Interior Design and Production: Kelly Doudna, Mighty Media, Inc.
Photo Credits: iStockphoto, Shutterstock

Library of Congress Cataloging-in-Publication Data

Doudna, Kelly, 1963-
 Mischievous mosquitoes / Kelly Doudna.
    p. cm. -- (Bug books)
 ISBN 978-1-61783-193-5
 1. Mosquitoes--Juvenile literature. I. Title.
 QL536.D66 2012
 595.77'2--dc23
                 2011023466

SandCastle™ Level: Transitional

SandCastle™ books are created by a team of professional educators, reading specialists, and content developers around five essential components—phonemic awareness, phonics, vocabulary, text comprehension, and fluency—to assist young readers as they develop reading skills and strategies and increase their general knowledge. All books are written, reviewed, and leveled for guided reading, early reading intervention, and Accelerated Reader® programs for use in shared, guided, and independent reading and writing activities to support a balanced approach to literacy instruction. The SandCastle™ series has four levels that correspond to early literacy development. The levels are provided to help teachers and parents select appropriate books for young readers.

Emerging Readers
(no flags)

Beginning Readers
(1 flag)

Transitional Readers
(2 flags)

Fluent Readers
(3 flags)

Contents

Mischievous Mosquitoes 4
Find the Mosquito 22
Glossary 24

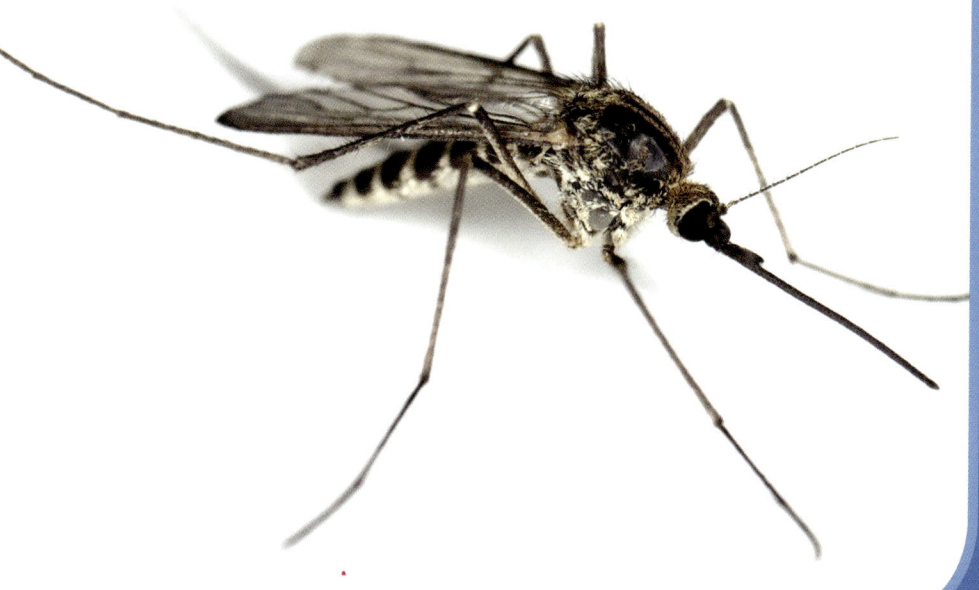

Mischievous Mosquitoes

Mosquitoes are small. They are less than ½ inch (1.25 cm) long.

Mosquitoes have big eyes. They cover most of their heads.

Mosquitoes have two **antennae**. **Male** mosquitoes have long hairs on their antennae.

Mosquitoes have two wings.
Their wings have lines.
The lines are called **veins**.

Mosquitoes fly to look for food. They can fly for four hours at a time.

Mosquitoes have six legs.
Their legs are long and skinny.

Male mosquitoes eat **nectar** from flowers. They don't bite people.

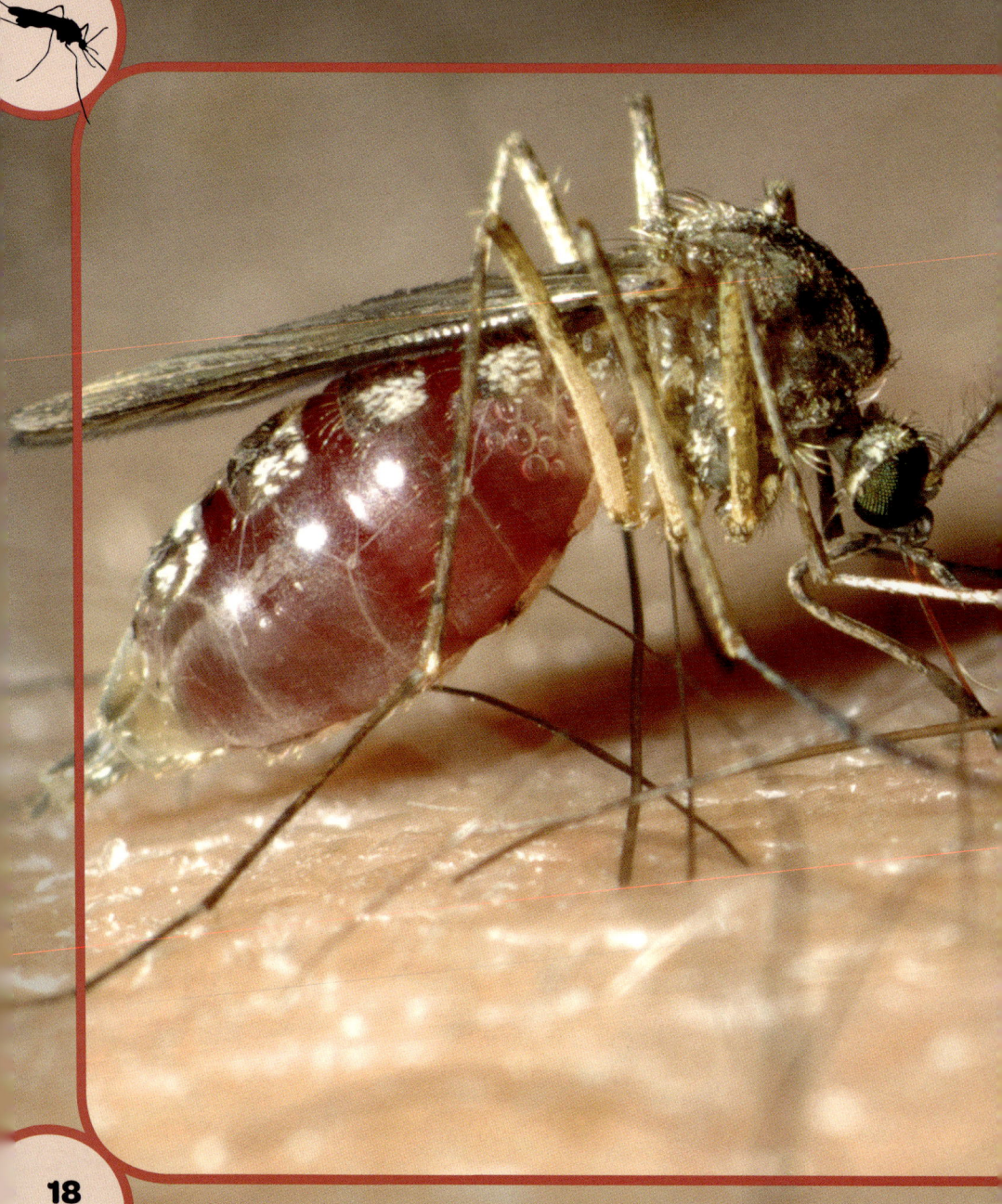

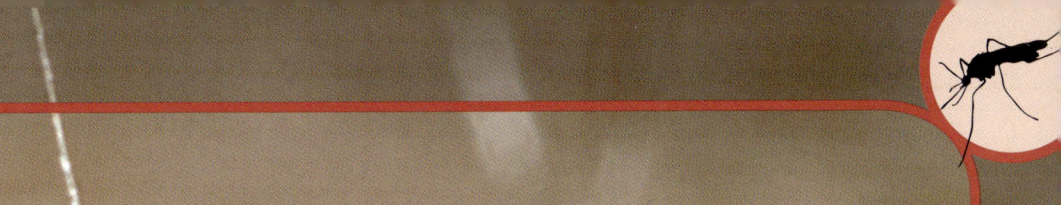

Female mosquitoes eat **nectar** and blood. They need the blood to make eggs.

Eating makes the mosquito's body fatter. Its body can **change** color too.

Find the Mosquito

A

B

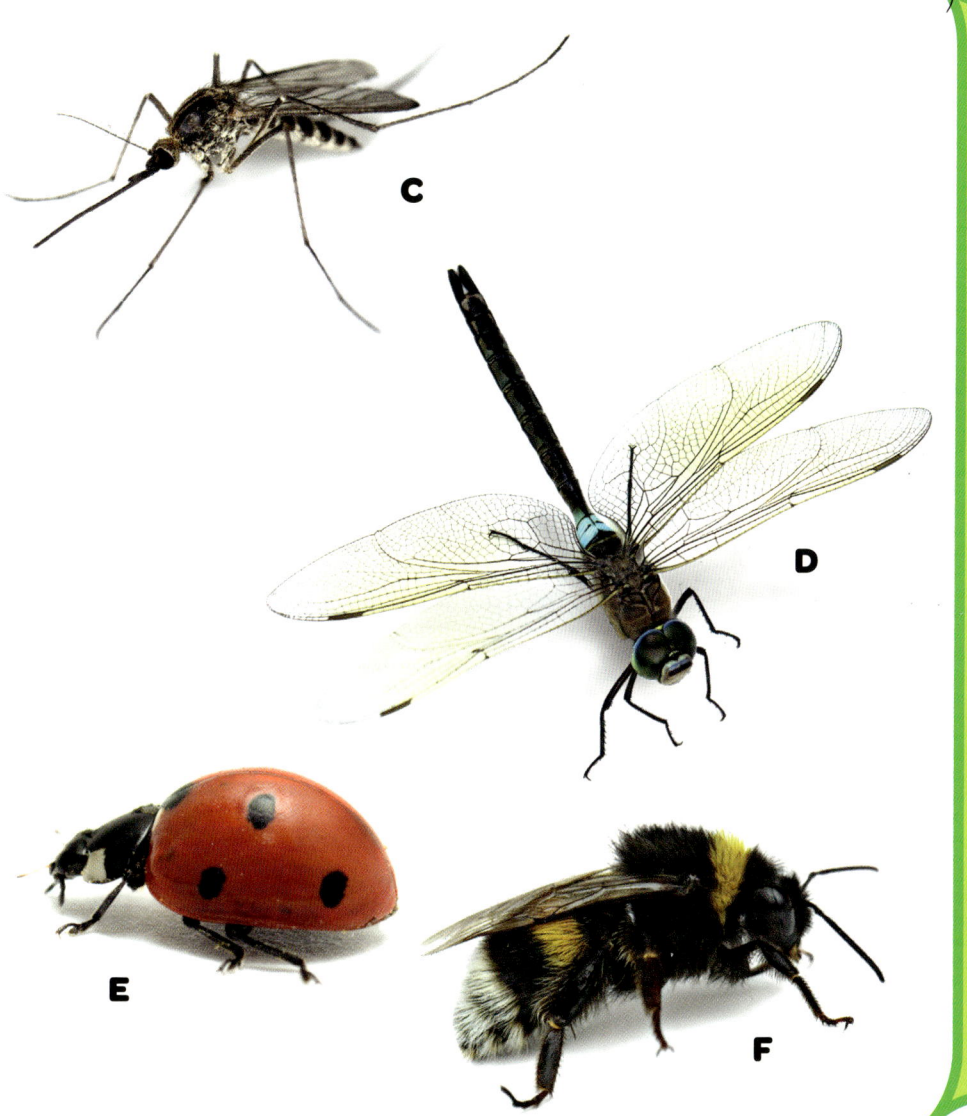

Answer: C

Glossary

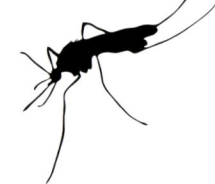

antenna – a feeler on an insect's head.

change – to become different.

female – being of the sex that can produce eggs or give birth. Mothers are female.

male – being of the sex that can father offspring. Fathers are male.

nectar – a sweet liquid found in flowers.

vein – one of the lines of thick material that make an insect's wing stiff.